84 STORIES
84 WORDS

84
STORIES

84
WORDS

from the

N°84

WRITING GROUP

First published in Great Britain in 2019 by No.84 Writing Group

ISBN: 9781073567676

Concept by Adrian Flaherty
Organisation by Sally Skeptic
Edited by Pinar Galip and Jonathan Fryer
Designed & typeset by David John Griffin

Printed by kdp

Foreword

Thank you for at least picking up this anthology of very short stories. We hope that if this is where you have started reading this book, you will carry on to the best bit, the work contributed by the ladies and gentlemen who have had a brush with the No.84 writers' social known as '84 Words'. A place where writers at every stage of the evolutionary scale come to chat, drink tea and even sometimes write a little. Sometimes as little as 84 words.

The challenge of each of these pieces of work is to engage you enough to maybe make you think, or at least pause. Unconventional in size and remarkably simple, think of these collected stories as a selection box where there is something for everyone, but not every one will be for you. We hope they might amuse, entertain and on occasion creep you out a little, but they never last long. They are short, easily consumed and moreish, like Don Estelle and David Hamilton.

We would like to thank everyone who has contributed to this publication. It has been a pleasure working with you all, meandering through the winding prompts and uncovering the plethora of ways it was possible to interpret a word like 'Fringe' in 84 words. The spread of subject matter within these pages is testimony to the imagination and creativity of all the authors. Trying to tell a story in eighty four words is not straightforward, so enjoy yourself while you marvel at their talent.

No.84

Contributors

When the idea of this book was first mooted some of the amazing people who have come and talked to audiences at No.84 were invited to contribute and, sportingly, several agreed. Additionally writers who weren't part of the Gravesend group were asked if they would support the project and a number came up trumps. They supported on the flimsiest of briefs: 'any subject, any genre, any style'. Thank you to them for supporting this fun, creative venture and for extending the range of authorship.

The Word Count

The word count is very simplistic – ask Microsoft® Word for the answer. In the counting it handles word hyphenation, an em dash or an en dash with aplomb but occasionally the insertion of a non-standard character can upset the count algorithm. The end result is a final check by a human who concedes to imperfection – especially when the task is counting 84-words, 84 times – so if you find an 85th word, or just 83, please be kind and keep very, very quiet about it.

CONTENTS

84

by **Keith Avenue**

81... 82...

The counting had become monotonous and Annabella was getting bored.

83...

It had taken what felt like ages to get to this point and some time ago she had had the thought that maybe the hiders might have settled in and were also bored.

One hundred seemed a long way away from where she was and her mind wandered. What if when she opened her eyes everything was different?

She thought she should hurry up just in case it might be.

84...

A Cautionary Tale

by **Kat Arney**

"I'm not saying you're wrong, I'm just saying I don't think this is the right way," the woman sighed, squelching thick mud beneath her Wellingtons as she shifted under the heavy backpack.

"Give that here," he snapped, snatching the map with a gloved hand and heading down the overgrown path. "Scientific research shows that women just aren't as good at spatial awareness and navigation."

"Suit yourself," she muttered under her breath, watching from a careful distance as he fell headfirst into a well, actually.

A Measure of Hate

by **Matt Hill**

"This loft is hell to get into!" I exclaimed. Ten minutes in our new house and I was already finding fault.

"The hatch doesn't open properly, the ladder's broken, and once it's down it's too close to the sink. I have to climb over the loo. We'll never get our boxes up there," I continued, as Kay entered the bathroom.

"And to think the husband played train sets up there," Kay replied, raising an eyebrow. I laughed.

"He must have really hated his wife."

A Perfect Crime Scene

by **Paul Hiscock**

The Earl's place at the breakfast table had been meticulously prepared. Ranks of shining cutlery, pristine ivory plates, a delicate porcelain cup and a crisply folded newspaper lay on the starched white tablecloth.

Beside the table, the Earl's body had been carefully placed on a claret coloured rug that perfectly matched the blood soaking into it. The knife used to stab him had been polished to a gleam and returned to its proper place with the silverware.

It was obvious the butler did it.

A Trip in 1977

by **Sue Couves**

We circled the Echo Square roundabout for no other reason than we could.

The night air was crisp and a full moon illuminated the sky with thousands of sparkling diamonds.

The turning circle on Kathy's clapped out convertible Cortina leant itself to the circular motion and the vodka, and a joint or two, or maybe three, and those tabs just before we left the party were working wonderful, crazy miracles.

I dreamily closed my eyes on the beauty of life as the juggernaut struck.

Anti-social Behaviour

by **Matt Hill**

"No more *Happy Pig*!" boomed Greg as he raised his glass.

"Yeah," Andy agreed, "that pub had to go."

"We'll be fined, of course," continued Greg, "but that's nowt compared to the profits we'll make on the flats."

Without warning, the front of the kitchen collapsed, leaving Greg and Andy staring at a mechanical digger. Steve Jones, ex-landlord of *The Happy Pig* was behind the wheel. He laughed with glee as he inched the digger into the kitchen.

"See how you like it, morons!"

Aperture

by **P Zakia**

The first fumes of dusk brought all woodland ramblings to an end.

Summer rites were conducted in the haystack warmth of July, witches summoned and evil spirits banished with sticks torn from thickets.

There, in the rectory wall, gold light oozed from an opening catching her attention.

She put her eye to it: dark, ivied trees stood mutely against the hollow tock of a woodpecker.

"Julia!"

She dashed from the hole – mother calling.

From the mossy silence, a tiny hand waved from the hole.

Arrivals

by **Keith Avenue**

He thought he was in the back of a van; perhaps a Transit or that type of thing. He couldn't make it out through the weave of the sacking that covered him but there seemed a lot of space as he rolled and slid around the vehicle as it surged forward quickly.

He figured he would miss his flight now and started to wonder what she would think when he didn't show from the arrivals gate as she had asked him to by email.

Button

by **Cathy Clement**

Nothing happened.

She pushed it again and, again, nothing happened.

There was a pause while she thought about what was happening and she pushed again, then repeatedly until it became clear nothing was happening. She pushed another button, then another and then two at the same time.

Still nothing happened.

She ran her fingers over the panel pressing as many buttons as she could and let out a little frustrated groan. The doors slid slowly to a close. She pushed the button.

Nothing happened.

Courage

by **Mike Swift**

Courage takes many different forms. Facing an enemy; conquering a phobia; battling illness. Derek's fear was no less real but, for him, took all of his reserves of courage. He climbed the steps to the front door and entered hesitantly. The girl smiled at him from behind a desk and invited him to take a seat.

"You can go up now," the words he dreaded to hear.

He was met by an attractive white-coated young woman.

"Just a check-up today, Mr Jones. No toothache?"

Courage on an Anniversary

by **David John Griffin**

It was the day of Donald and Margaret's second wedding anniversary. Donald, sprawled on the sofa in his usual position, opened a can of lager and shouted, "Cheers!"

Margaret drew in breath, finally willing courage and determination for what was needed to be said.

"Donald, listen carefully," she yelled, "You are nothing but a lazy, boring man. We never go out; you hardly speak to me. I'm leaving you."

"Good," he replied simply, with no courage needed. "Turn the TV on before you leave."

Delicious

by **Cathy Clement**

"It has a mouth feel of something fleshy. Sausage fleshy rather than melon fleshy, but not savoury or salty in any way.

"It's not... not sweet, not comforting like a caramel or intriguing like a pepper, and you wouldn't want it with ice-cream or to accompany bitter coffee.

"Let me have another piece.

"It's delicious... It enrobes the tongue and delights the back of the nose and throat. It's unctuous enough to attach to the teeth yet light on the pallet...

"What is it?"

Eighty-Four

by **Richard Wall**

He stared at her across the table; as beautiful now as she was in 1940.

Arthritic fingers shook as he read the perfume-scented letter. Eyes welled at the words she had written on her 84th birthday in 2004.

The sentiments of a young girl, trapped in the cancer scrawl of a breathing cadaver.

He took the tablets from his pocket, stirred each one into the teacup, looked across at the empty chair, smiled for the last time and lifted the teacup to his lips.

Elliot Delivers Groceries

by **David John Griffin**

Elliot loads his bicycle basket with groceries for the manor. He rides enthusiastically along the empty road on a windy day.

The wind ceases, then an eerie silence descends. The stench of rotting fruit wafts from the basket. Ghostly fingers prod his ribs.

Now he sees a vision of a Victorian shop with bottle glass windows, where a terraced house should be. In front of it, a stick of a man sways, candle wax for eyes and purple skin, mouthing the words, "Go back!"

Extraordinary Event

by **David John Griffin**

The moon cast a ghostly white light over the snow on the plain. The woods beyond stood hushed in the chill air.

A huge tiger, its stripes pulsing as if made of neon, padded slowly across the snow towards the shack in the middle of the field. Condensation emitted from its snorting nostrils.

Inside the shack, Angus looked through binoculars to track the progress of the animal. He turned hurriedly, shook his wife by the shoulder and said, "Wake up, Joan, you're dreaming again."

Farming Philosophy

by **Ben Morton**

It has been a bumper year in the Devon countryside, the weather has been wet in spring, warm in summer and the harvest was clear and dry. Two old farmers lean on the fence and look at their overflowing barns, their well-fed sheep and cattle and their groaning storehouses.

"Well", says one. "Would you look at that lot. I've no more bloody room."

"Ar", says the other, "and if them barns goes up in smoke, it'll be the worse year I've ever bloody known."

Football and Flowers

by **Sam Jewiss**

Serena was walking along Strawberry Lane, trying to fight the swarm of excited Newcastle United fans on their way to St James' Park when suddenly they all freeze. She was looking around in bewilderment when the Greek goddess Chloris materialized in front of her.

"You would make a beautiful shrub," Chloris declared and promptly turned Serena into a pink and white viburnum.

Chloris smiled at her creation and unfroze the populace as she disappeared.

The beautiful viburnum was immediately trampled by unknowing football fans.

Ghost

by **Peter Germany**

The girl woke up suddenly, fear sweeping across her. At the foot of her bed was her older brother as clear as day. She screamed so hard she couldn't spcak the next morning.

Their mother came running into the room in her nightdress and hair in curlers. She too saw her son and scrcamed. Her son was in Burma, fighting for King and country. But she saw him there, at the bottom of her daughter's bed, as clear as day.

Was this a message?

Gift Horse

by **Matt Hill**

The man on the doorstep was drenched. Rain had soaked his clothes but he still managed a smile as Tina opened the door.

"Hello," he said, "we're collecting for the old-people's home. Can you spare anything?"

Tina smiled. "Wait here, I have just the thing." She closed the door and returned to the lounge where her obnoxious grandfather sat in his favourite chair. He'd dropped his lunch and was swearing at the TV.

"Hey Grandad," Tina called. "Get your coat. You're going on holiday!"

Happy Christmas Passengers!

by **Judith Northwood-Boorman**

"Not another French air traffic controllers' strike! They really pick their moments…"

Tempers are rising in the jam-packed, over-crowded, steamy Gatwick departure lounge. The insistent shrieking of over-tired children and babies adding to the tangible stress levels.

In Paris, Jean-Claude, laden with presents, steps across his threshold.

"Jean-Claude!" exclaims Chantal, "I wasn't expecting you home until tomorrow. Wonderful!"

"I just had to stir up a few grievances, ma chérie. It works a dream, every time! There's no way I could miss our family Christmas."

Hearing Aide

by **Jayne Curtis**

"Darling, please don't talk to my handbag."

"Well, put them in then!"

"In a minute, I'm just having a rest. It's noisy." His stern look I'd seen before. "Okay, okay. What were you saying?"

At various points in my husband's life he has spoken to the sink, the downstairs loo, the upstairs loo, the car door, the cup holder, his inside pocket, the coffee table, the lounge carpet, but mostly the handbag. I know it annoys him... but... selective hearing is a beautiful thing!

Hello Beastie

by **Kayleigh Manley**

"She's gone." Linda cried.
"I know," sobbed Mandy, "awful news."
"I'll miss her."
"Me too."

I feel my insides wriggle.

"Twenty years we were friends."
"Best friends."

My teeth itch.

"Shame we fell out."
"Well, she was difficult."
"Guess she got what she deserved."
"Agreed."

Nasty spiteful hypocrites!
I silence its voice. Breathe.

"What do you think, Cas?"
I shrug. "Didn't know her."
"Lucky you!"

They laugh.
The beast growls.
I submit…
Feeding time.
> *Don't worry, ladies.*
> *You'll be seeing your friend real soon.*

Hole

by **Keith Avenue**

He found a hole and hid in it. It seemed like the thing to do as he was in her bedroom without being invited or dressed. He could see one of his shoes on the outer edge of a pile of hers and considered trying to collect it before she came through the door but thought it was much less risky to stay where he was.

He watched the door in silence.

From beside him in the dark he heard a voice.

"Hello Tony…"

Hospital Radio 1995

by **Mark Whitehouse**

He means well. I know he does.

Unfortunately his appearance suggests a greater commitment to community service than musical discovery.

"*Isn't She Lovely?*" he offers.
"Of course she is," I smile, "but that song feels… over familiar."
"*Unforgettable?*"
"In every way, but I want something that's modern and sublime."

Wildly misguided, he plays his trump, "*Can You Feel The Love Tonight?*"

And in that moment – my beautiful, newborn daughter nestled neatly in my arms – I realise:
I've Never Known A Girl Like You Before.

Hot Chick

by **P Zakia**

He spied her out, with that sultry jaywalk across the street. A mouth-watering slow wiggle: clearly a taunt.

Chest out, breast exposed, flaunting. A ruffle of oil-slick feathers trimming her neckline. She idled by the gutter, spying a semi-smoked cigarette butt on the pavement and half contemplates picking it up. Her type gets bored easily – she loses interest and struts past.

Again that booty shake.

He keeps to the wall, creeping up on her.

POUNCE!

A mouth full of feathers.
She asked for it.

Immigrant

by **Peter Germany**

It was 7pm. The Victoria Sponge was stale, but had more life in it than the immigrant that was lying dead on the floor of my Tea Room.

I'm an immigrant, so is my wife, from a country where war was raging so I know death when I see it.

The dead man had travelled all this way, the right way; not hiding in lorries or travelling on a kiddies' dinghy, only to have a heart attack when he finally found his son: me.

It Rained

by **Peter Germany**

It rained. Hard. Harder than I'd seen it in a good five years. Roads that never flooded were turned into rivers as drains were overwhelmed from this onslaught by Mother Nature. If the council had coughed up to clean them out it wouldn't be this bad.

People took shelter where they could; even those who had the sense to pick up coats and umbrellas were having to halt their journeys.

I watched all this from my home office with my mug of hot chocolate.

Jennifer

by **Matt Hill**

She was as beautiful as I remembered. How long had it been – ten, twelve years? The time had passed in a blur. Perhaps it was twenty years since I'd last set eyes on her? Age does strange things with our memories. You think you'll have them forever, but they all eventually fade. Life was cruel. Yet here she was, looking lovelier than ever and back in my life again.

I turned the ignition key and the engine roared into life.

"Hello Jennifer," I said.

Ladysmith Black Mambazo

by **P Zakia**

With squat legs planted like strong pillars, she keens. Her waters break, an amniotic stream gushes into the thirsting dust of an African dawn.

Tall trees with sparse thatches exhale.
Beetle and ant stand witness, holding their breath.
   The sun, pregnant with a new day, beams
   yellow blessings.

A last struggle, a twist of gut and release. Grey wrinkled flesh steams in the morning haze.

A protective circle of matriarchal love congregates around this new child of Africa.
Trunks rise and bellow with praise.

Lampposts

by **Cathy Clement**

Damp and a little more out of breath than he was comfortable with, Andrew rested his weight against the kitchen wall. A sopping wet feeling made him aware of what was in his pocket. As he pushed against it he felt it ooze and a trickle of something recently warm made contact with his skin.

"I can't believe it."

He moved to the window and looked out into the car park, where the poorly lit drizzle beneath the lampposts had begun to form puddles.

Lashings of Custard

by **David John Griffin**

A restaurant customer sat inspecting his pie and custard with suspicion. He waved at the waiter.

"This isn't good enough," he said.

"What do you mean sir?" the puzzled waiter replied.

"The menu item specifically says pie with lashings of custard. There's only two spoonfuls of custard here."

"Sir," the waiter replied, "I'll tell the chef."

A minute later, the chef bustled though from the kitchen, holding a large saucepan.

"Here's your lashings," he cried out, pouring the saucepan's contents over the customer's head.

Last Memories

by **David John Griffin**

Searing pain through the skull, mauve filter, dizziness.

I'm in a red clay pit. Shadows sharp and black, fierce sun pressing. I wear some sort of uniform with a radio contraption crackling.

A metallic device in that corner, buried in the earth wall. Two wires exposed like an insect's antennae, pulsing.

I seem to have wire clippers in my hand – must be a puzzle to solve, a test maybe.

Then it's easy; although my hand is trembling for some reason, I'll clip those wires.

Liar Bird

by **Em Dehaney**

Professor Pendleton clung to the slippery bark, her eyes stinging with sweat. She had been tracking the bird the locals called *loro tramposa* for months, and now almost one hundred feet up above the canopy, she was sure she had it in her sights.

The famed parrot of the genus *Amazona mendax* had been declared extinct centuries ago, if it had ever existed at all.

One oily, black feather would be the making of her career.

Now if she could just reach that branch…

Monologue

by **Keith Avenue**

"...and then we want him to turn to the crowd and recite a monologue to introduce all the carers of our heroine and make note of their special talents. One is medically trained, one is upbeat and another has allergies. You know they all have something."

"Got it, I think I understand. What about:

There once was a man from the North,
Who planned to wed a dwarf.
He ate lots of cabbage, to slim for the marriage
And is known as 'Breezy' henceforth."

Mummy Smell

by **Paolo Viscardi**

Morning rush hour, crammed on a tram. An unexpected perfume catches my attention – the aroma of an Egyptian mummy.

It's rather disconcerting.

Complex and distinctive, the deep, musky, spicy scent has a sweetness that fades to a slightly bitter end, almost like mince pies and Earl Grey tea.

I scan the other passengers searching for the source, but nothing unusual stands out from the damp, overcoated figures around me. Then I feel stick-thin fingers grasp my shoulder from behind.

Never desecrate a tomb.

My Life So Far

by **Sue Couves**

My life so far, from what I see
through my selective memory:
a learning curve with no straight line,
an erratic path – no clear sign
shackled by disability
masked behind my vanity.
The strength and love of family.
Nothing has been by my design.
My life so far.
Thwarted ambitions not to be
My success is the child born from me,
Perfectly formed this girl divine,
A beautiful life made from mine,
The fruit of love – this growing tree,
anchoring the roots
of reality.

No Looking Back

by **Sue Couves**

Her flight from Africa had been arduous, dangerous and exhausting. The meeting with others had been successful and now she waits patiently, holed up in the Norfolk fens watching, and scheming the lies, deceit and murder that will undoubtedly follow.

Many of her river neighbours have been busy home-making, but suddenly her lazy body starts to full alertness.

Opportunity arises and she strikes within seconds.

Gulp down their offspring's egg, lay her own and depart.

There is no looking back for the non-maternal cuckoo.

Number 84

by **Sally Skeptic**

The first cryptic crossword clue she'd solved had been thrown out by her father: "Television programme we back."

She responded with her favourite type of programme, "Western."

"Of course," and he wrote it in explaining the connection between '*we back*' and '*western*'. That's when the crossword bug bit.

Clue: A poisonous elemental number is a game with one in with the miners. A game – 'polo'? Then the miners' union the NUM. Put one in there to get 'nium'. Together 'polonium'.

Element **Number Eighty Four**!

Openings

by **Kayleigh Manley**

He woke, confused, shivering.

His breath clouded upon hitting the frigid air. Beeswax candles illuminated the tomb, a coffin lay beside him: dark oak cocooned with cobwebs.

Startled, he fell from the altar. Human bones crunched underfoot. Panic ensued.

"Trapped!" he thought, "there has to be an exit!"

He searched.

"A crack! A crack in the bricks!"

With hope, he clawed at the stone, but dainty fingernails are no match for concrete.

Fingernails bleeding, splintered, he persevered unaware of the casket opening behind him.

Our Seasalter Holiday in Gran's Charabanc

by **Brenda Moss**

Gran handed us a white enamel bucket, saying, trustingly, "Stay together. Fetch your tea. The tide's out".

We crossed the rickety bridge over the stream, our spades furiously unearthing cockles. Winkles were knifed off rocks. Yesterday's kite flying and cricket forgotten.

The dragged laden bucket left a grooved snail's trail in the sand.

Soon cockles were bubbling on the Calor gas stove.

Contentedly eating cockle sandwiches, black beauty spots from the winkles on our sunburned faces, my brothers and I smiled at one another.

Parrot

by **Peter Germany**

They taught me to mimic their words, to abuse a naturally evolved defence system that took more time to develop than their puny minds could comprehend. I should flee and soar on the winds of the free world but I know I wouldn't last out there; out in this ugly, chaotic, poisonous, colourless jungle they've created around them.

Damn them for what they have done to this once great world. Damn them and their need to destroy all they see.

Damn them.

Ooo, crackers!

Parrot Strikes Back

by **Matt Hill**

"Don't you bloody well answer me back!" screamed Mr Marsh. Rage was popping out of his contorted red face.

Gary Blake stared at him, calm and composed.

"Don't you bloody well answer me back!" Gary replied as he turned to grin at his friends.

There was an audible intake of breath from everyone else in the room. Gary laughed, not even trying to hide it. Mr Marsh looked like he would explode.

"Right. That's it. I've had enough, you smart-arse little parrot! Come here!"

Pecan Pie

by **Em Dehaney**

Pecan pie crumbs stuck to her cheek as she rolled over and reached for the remote. Lifting her arm sent a forgotten chocolate wrapper floating to the floor. She ignored it and carried on staring at the television. The talking heads yammered away, saying nothing.

Flick. Flick. Flick.

Click.

The metal of the gun barrel was cold on her skin; even through her matted hair. He had found her. After all these years hidden away in the dark. What a waste of a life.

People

by **Dom Sullivan**

It's a good thing that I like people-watching, otherwise this job could be very dull: operating the city CCTV cameras endlessly and watching the world pass by. Most don't realise they are being watched, but the ones that do tend to stand out from the crowd.

Here is one now.

The classic head down, hood up and avoiding others. Really, who does he think he is, Jason Bourne? Maybe a druggie, thief or mugger?

No chance – just a shy idiot walking into a lamppost.

Priest

by **Peter Germany**

Daniel Duncan Daniels was arrested for impersonating a priest this morning in Gravesend. He is forty-two years old and has a receding hairline and stands at five feet six inches tall.

He was arrested while attempting to remove all the sacramental wine from the vestry, and had all but one box in his car when the Reverend Kevin Morris and Sister Agatha pulled up to Daniels' Morris Minor at the church.

When asked why he was stealing the wine he simply said, "Feck off!"

Regret

by **Sally Skeptic**

He's waiting for the 17:48 – seat guaranteed by his first-class ticket.

Another train arrives; a young man alights and runs into the arms of a similar youth on the platform. They hug and kiss tenderly.

The older man tuts, looks disapproving, expects support from those around but the tide has turned and his fellow travellers do not share his prejudice.

His thoughts turn to his wonderful wife and then to Michael, from forty years ago and inwardly he weeps for his true lost love.

Riot

by **David John Griffin**

Trees lining a stream lean to see their reflection. Takeda's attention is taken from boulders streaked with moss, to chains swinging under the bridge.

The samurai kneels in a frozen state, the blade of his sword catching light.

Shouts from further upstream.

Within stained swirls of water, a kimono drifts; gold and crimson silk pulsing and billowing as if an organic creature, alive.

Takeda's bare head falls forward as if in prayer, then he grasps the ornate sword handle and stands.

It is time.

Scrape

by **Cathy Clement**

It itched.

It really itched and his stubby chewed-back fingernails could not just get enough purchase to feel as if they were doing any good at all. Looking around the room he could identify a few things with enough edge to make a scrape equal to the itch that penetrated deep through the flesh, but nothing had the reach required. In desperation, he opened a window and positioned himself against the frame whilst leaning on the sill.

His parents never understood why he jumped.

Searing Day

by **George Brooker**

Too much before even getting out of bed.

September had been removed from calendars, making the gap between Christmases shorter. In a bid to improve public health, vouchers were given to those who walked to shops instead of going online. A Twitter poll decided the punishment of a paedophile caught by a vigilante group.

Her feet made it to the ground before lunchtime, luckily, finding a reason or a will or a something else to move.

"This will be another Happy Day. Searing Day?"

Shadows

by **Keith Avenue**

From her bed in the corner she could see everything in her room by just turning her head, but only if they closed the door when they left. She liked it if they left the door open when they were in the room, though sometimes it felt cosy if they sat on the bed when it was dark and the door was closed. When the door was open she could see shadows but couldn't see if they were hiding in the corner until later.

She Left

by **Catriona Murfitt**

There was a genuine smile on her face, a feeling of exhilaration, a new adventure.

Her aged skin and aching bones had slipped away. She could just make out the faces of loved ones saying goodbye. See the light of their souls shine like beacons, light that now seemed trapped, made dim in clumsy bodies.

But she was free, shining brightest bright.

She sent them her love with the message 'I'll be with you again' and walked into the warmth of her mother's embrace.

Sick

by **Cathy Clement**

I got up, called in sick and put the telly on.

I thought about making tea but thought that the milk was probably too old to be of any use, which meant I probably wouldn't eat either unless I ate some cereal dry.

The heating was off and my bare legs could feel the difference in the air temperature between the living room and beneath the duvet. I could have an effect on this but probably won't.

I'll just watch the telly. That's best.

Stranger on the Train

by **David John Griffin**

The man in the train carriage engaged Mr Summers in conversation.

"Nice to meet you, again," said the stranger, extending a hand.

"I'm sorry," Mr Summers said, "I don't recall meeting you before."

The stranger gave a disturbing smile – a strange, devilish grin, exposing grey, pointed teeth.

"Where are you travelling to?" he asked, retracting his hand.

Mr Summers was reluctant to speak but finally said, "Stratford."

"No, you're not," the stranger replied, and the train entered a tunnel with a squeal of wheels.

Support

by **Peter Germany**

This is why supportive people are my favourite thing; they encourage others to follow their dreams and never belittle them or their dreams.

They know what it's like to have such passion and drive and love seeing other people doing what they love.

Supportive people inspire others to follow their own dreams and can take courage from seeing them succeed in their lives.

They never tear you down, they never talk down to you; all they want to see is everyone fulfilling their dreams.

Tea for Two?

by **Paolo Viscardi**

Sam walked into the tearoom and looked at the menu. Words swam like ants in a gutter, distorted by welling tears.

Beginnings, middles and ends are for stories – they're narrative games that we try to play with reality, but which fall flat on closer inspection. Life is lived in the middle of our first-person narrative and we are born telling our story alone, but sometimes miracles happen and we have the joy of narrating in first person plural.

"Pot of tea. Two cups please!"

Tea for Two? Reprise

by **Paolo Viscardi**

Sam walked into the tearoom and looked at the menu. Words swam like ants in a gutter, distorted by welling tears.

Beginnings, middles and ends are for stories – narrative games that we try to play with reality, but which fall flat on closer inspection. Life is lived in the middle of our first-person narrative, but there are few greater joys than narrating in first person plural and truly few sorrows greater than switching back to the singular.

"Pot of tea, please. Just one cup."

Territorial

by **P Zakia**

"Go! Go! Go!"
You bark the command. All four dash from their posts through the water-logged forest, flinging mud-spatter.

Five-fingered palms smack them in the face. Entrails of ivy and fern, grabby, resistant. Mission objective: locate and retrieve. Sights, smells and sounds merge with intel from the recon. It's near, very near. Five-clicks north.

They pant white-hot desperation.
     Delirium.
          Where?
          Where?

Minutes later, one grinds to a halt, ears scissoring to attention.
A pink ball falls to your feet with a squeak.

Mission complete.

That Christmas Feeling

by **Ben Morton**

"Food, glorious food! Rum ti tum ti tum fills my belly and expands my bum!"

"What are you on about, Nick?"

"It's time for food, my little elfin friend. Vittles, scran, nosh!"

"Oh, right, come on then, the market's just round the corner."

"Street food. Fabulous! Oodles of noodles, curry and rice and all things nice! Or a roast pork roll or maybe…"

"No, it's a Christmas market Santa, mulled wine, cake, loads of mince pies. Santa, you alright? You've gone really green. Santa?"

The Apple

by **Sue Couves**

There on the table sat a magnificent example of an English Cox's apple waiting on his mother to fetch the water jug from the kitchen to complete her still life painting arrangement.

It shone beautifully, buffed to perfection and perfectly poised to reflect the light, and Freddy stared longingly at the scarlet, inviting skin. His mouth ran juices, sluicing over a tongue that he knew would not be satiated until it tasted the sweet forbidden flesh.

He bit hard and the maggot was halved.

The Architect

by **Sally Skeptic**

Could the architect design a moat around the enclosure so there would be no visual barrier between the elephants and the humans? Of course the architect could.

There was praise for the design from the architectural elite and the visitors loved the idea. Until the day the oldest elephant overbalanced on the edge, fell in and was firmly trapped.

The best efforts of the emergency services couldn't save him.

The architect wept, destroyed the plans and accolades and subsequently designed only brutalist tower blocks.

The Beggar

by **Sue Couves**

The rain lashed down relentlessly, bouncing tiny beads off shining London pavements and gurgling down barely coping, grey-grated drain covers. Rivulets of running water channelled by worn kerb stones attempt to contain the rushing and rising, the rinsing and spinning of small leaves, cigarette butts and the tutt of discarded flotsam that reveal the wastefulness of our throwaway lives.

The bedraggled beggar shelters a scrawny dog under his oversized anorak and wishes he was home under the warmth and comfort of the Syrian sun.

The Beginning

by **Mike Swift**

It was just such a simple moment in time, eyes meeting eyes across a crowded bar. Hers were hazel, mine as dark as night with hidden depths.

She smiled so sweetly. Would she have done so had she known what the future held for her?

I think not.

I watched as she drifted towards the door on impossibly high heels, hips swaying provocatively. The darkness of the winter night swallowed her, masking me from her sight as I followed silently.

The stalking had begun.

The Box

by **Lex H. Jones**

Darla had expected the box to be black, not grey.

Being grey made it worse, somehow. Black would have been striking, as it should be when you received the box on your doorstep. Grey made it mundane, a part of modern life – which, of course, it now was.

With a heavy sigh, she brought the box inside her home.

It happened as soon as she closed the door. She didn't scream though. It was important what the neighbours thought of her family, after all.

The Chair

by **Wendy Bretherton**

Emily's cafe chair was vacant.

Someone whispered she'd gone away. A muttered hint of a husband betrayal and wasn't it strange that Mrs Miniver was missing too.

Surely Emily must have known, after all. Wasn't it obvious, the amount of time they'd spent together sprucing up Mrs Miniver's vegetable patch down the allotment. And that lovely new garden of Emily's, why the flower beds had all been redone and raised.

The new roses look absolutely stunning and how strange one is called Mrs Miniver.

The Collector

by **David John Griffin**

"Drat," Jeremy said, while turning the key in the car a third time.

He got out and walked along the dark, country road to a cottage. The garden was overgrown and there were car keys scattered over the path.

He knocked loudly. An old man, holding a knife, opened the door.

Jeremy asked, "Sorry to bother, but can I use your phone? I've run out of petrol."

"Certainly," the man replied and stabbed Jeremy in the heart. "Another one for my collection," he said.

The Great Escape

by **Jonathan Fryer**

If only I could escape.

I can't be stuck in here for much longer – it's been months!

So cramped.

There must be more to life than this. Surely.

If I could just break free from this damp and claustrophobic prison…

I need a plan. Now.

Wait! A break through! There IS light at the end of the tunnel.

One final push. Come on. The end's in sight.

Success! Freedom! Time to cry – loudly.

Now everyone is going to notice me.

A new life awaits.

The Lion

by **Sally Skeptic**

It was a very small zoo but it had a lion. A shabby, moth-eaten lion but a lion nonetheless.

It was standing near the back of its rather small cage when the boy, brave on his side of the bars, came and made faces at it and waggled his fingers tantalisingly close to the bars.

The lion looked sorrowfully at the boy. Then suddenly let out a loud, deep, terrifying roar. The boy, all colour drained from his face, beat a very hasty retreat.

The Map

by **Anthony Cowin**

The creases on the map divide the town with implausible borders, yet they built walls with each fold and flattened line. She wondered if she spilt her cranberry juice would it rain blood there.

She'd smoothed Sellotape over her street. Protection from spills and rips. She lay the map on the passenger seat.

Pain.

Her fingernail broke. She examined the damage. Her heart sank. The fractured nail had torn the tape away. Her house, her family home was now a hole in the paper.

The Miracle

by **Ros Fryer**

He lay in my arms, this tiny scrap of humanity.
His eyes open and try to focus on mine.

Skin so delicate, almost too soft to feel.
Downy hair covering the miniature, slightly
misshapen head.

His minuscule fingers wrapped around mine.
So helpless, so fragile, but so demanding.
Bending people to his every need.

His soft, little mouth opening and closing,
searching for nourishment.

My heart opened at the sight of this amazing
creation,
drawing him into my very soul.

My beautiful grandson, Sean.

The Old Lady and Home Help

by **David John Griffin**

"More tea, dear?" the old lady said, a sweet smile lighting her wrinkled face.

"No, really, thank you, Mrs Lighterman. I can't even finish this one," the new home help answered.

"But I insist," Mrs Lighterman said, pouring more tea into the cup parked on the coffee table. "Just like my departed husbands, you are."

'I won't drink it, it tastes bitter' and 'I don't feel at all well' were the last words thought by the home help as she collapsed onto the carpet.

The Park

by **Chrissie Pountain**

Most mornings, the dogs and girls walk through the park saying 'good morning,' but I never answer.

When I lived in London so many years ago I would have said 'hello' back, but now I keep quiet and still until they go away.

I was always a bit different. Nowadays they call it epilepsy, not insanity, so they put me in a hospital at Darenth Imbecile Asylum, miles away from my family. There I stayed and now, forever, in the graveyard.

Come tomorrow doggies.

The Tea Room at No. 84

by **Sue Couves**

84, what's in store? A gentle push of the door,
A slight creak to the floor, reveal me more, 84.

Bone china tea pots, with milk jugs and cups,
and saucers and spoons and solid coffee mugs.

Odd remnants of lives lived long, long ago,
Of loves and favourites and those just to show,
on Sundays.

Reminisce a past already written, the ink dry,
but where the sky to the future is blue, reflected
in mirrors true, that show the living core, of 84.

Thunder

by **Em Dehaney**

Red hair. Blue eyes. White skin. Black heart.

She scared the little kids revving up her motorbike. Thunder and white lightning. Made her mother cry. Made her daddy wonder what he had done to deserve such a daughter.

Didn't go to school. They didn't want her anymore. Kept herself busy with greased up bike chains and monkey wrench sets. Fingers always grubby, jeans a little worn at the knee.

But when she looked at me and smiled her crooked smile, it stopped my heart.

Two Frogs – A Romance

by **Ben Morton**

Green frog looked the other up and down, which didn't take long and then at the sky. "Seems like rain," he said.

Brown frog looked at him, which took longer and snaffled a passing fly. "So crunchy," she sighed.

"So dry," green frog agreed. "Rain would be exciting."

Brown frog turned a darker shade of mud. "Very exciting," she agreed and stared at green frog, who was becoming a delicate shade of blue green algae.

"If it rains," she said slowly, "that will mean…"

Us

by **Cathy Clement**

I'm finding that I'm thinking about everything I say and do.

I wonder if how I act will upset you, if I say or don't say something you might react in a way that makes me feel uncomfortable about myself.

I'm conscious of the fact that I'm often not being me because I'm not what you want and after everything else is completed I want to be wanted by you.

There are so many things to complete. Maybe the first thing will be us.

Van Gogh

by **Ben Morton**

In the Dutch town of Zundert lies the world's worst art museum.

The Van Gogh Huis's only paintings are poor modern copies; "In de geest van Van Gogh", nothing from the house he grew up in and room after room of empty arty space. Van Gogh was not about empty bloody space!

Fortunately, the mobile chippie is outside. Their van has his Potato Eaters as a mural, but these ones are happily wolfing down friet en mayonaise.

Proost! Van Gogh, eat your heart out!

Waiting

by **Keith Avenue**

Waiting in the car is the best bit.

Driving to get there is usually a little stressful, what with hold ups and traffic lights. There's a time frame, deadline thing about getting there that is just unpleasant.

Getting into the car is always work. Doors to unlock, bags to stow, weather to contend with. It's work.

The greet is rubbish: "How was your day?" and "Was the rain very wet?" The going back is usually dull.

Waiting in the car is the best bit.

Waiting in a Car

by **Matt Hill**

Tony sat in the driver's seat and glanced towards the bank.

"Come on," he whispered as he tapped his finger on the steering wheel.

The door of the bank opened and Gary stepped out. His rucksack was fit to burst.

"Quick," said Tony from the open car window. "Get in!"

Gary jogged over to the car, opened the back door and quickly threw himself inside.

"Well?" queried Tony.

"Nah mate," replied Gary. "We'll have to get rid of these rags at another clothes bank."

Wasteful Humans

by **P Zakia**

She hovered outside the department store, mesmerized by the agile movements of the statuesque blonde on the screen. This saturation of gold and bronze, this majestic statue doing its sultry stalk towards the camera. Gilded beads of sweat ran down her neck. Then, petulant and aggressive, she tore the gold choker from her neck. A powdery explosion of gold erupted on the floor.

She gasped. Sacrilege!

She took off in a flurry, navigating the currents, hugging the precious sacs of pollen to her body.

When I Grow Up

by **Peter Germany**

When I grow up I want to be an astronaut.

They go into space and look for aliens and they can see everyone in the whole world at the same time.

It would be really cool to go up in a rocket and then float around like I'm Superman. Then I could go out in a spacesuit and jump around on the moon, like they did in that old video I saw on YouTube. As long as I don't need to go toilet though.

Whisper

by **Cathy Clement**

It feels like the gentle seep of yolk when the membrane of a perfectly poached egg is breached and the orangey yellow semisolid escapes, at first quite quickly then slowing to a pace of ease and confidence.

It's that gentle gush of something viscous that coats anything in its wake, enhancing, rather than destroying the carrier and its collaborators in the way a condiment might with its violent and unpredictable splatters.

That's how it feels to me when you softly whisper 'I love you'.

Wolf Moon

by **Debra Frayne**

Staggering through the snow, his lips cannot contain his chattering teeth.

Hungry and exhausted, he trudges on; to stop is to perish. This exile will be the death of him but he has no choice.

The clouds break and the full moon illuminates the world.

He smiles. He is not finished.

Warmth spreads as his blood pumps new strength and energy through him. Tonight, he welcomes the change, wanting to live. He throws off his coat, dropping down to four paws, howling his survival.

Works Hard for the Money

by Matt Hill

Terry didn't enjoy his work but the pay was good and the hours fantastic; so few were necessary to do a good job.

He chuckled as he considered the effort required: a minute to respond to the text, five minutes to prepare, twenty to drive there and just two minutes to do the work.

Terry looked down at the limp body as dark blood pooled on the white lino. 'Five grand for half an hour,' he thought as he turned to leave. 'Easy money.'

Zen and the Art of Email

by **Anon**

Not all those invited to contribute an 84-word story felt able to accept the invitation but here's someone who declined with an 84-word reply. Since they'd clearly entered into the spirit of the activity I asked if, anonymised, it could be included and permission was given ... so here it is to finish the selection.

Hi Sally,

I am flattered that you liked my emails! I enjoyed yours too, what a fun time it was speaking in Gravesend.

I don't think I have the time to do this idea justice; as you say there's been a fair bit of running around on this end and it is creating a bit of a blockage. It doesn't look like it will slow down much for the next little while–so I must decline, but it's with a heavy heart!

Anon Speaker

Illustration by Fitzy:
Linea Portrait of No-One in 84 Individual Lines

CONTRIBUTORS' BIOGRAPHIES

THE WRITERS

Kat Arney
A Cautionary Tale
More about Kat
Kat is an award-winning science writer and broadcaster. She is the author of *Herding Hemingway's Cats: Understanding how our genes work* and *How to Code a Human,* and is the founder and director of First Create the Media – a multimedia communications consultancy for people who do science.

Find Kat on Twitter @Kat_Arney
Website: https://katarney.com/

Keith Avenue
84 : Arrivals : Hole : Monologue : Shadows : Waiting
More about Keith
Sagittarius

Wendy Bretherton
The Chair

George Brooker
Searing Day

Cathy Clement
Button : Delicious : Lampposts : Scrape : Sick : Us
: Whisper
More about Cathy
School Nurse until 1982 and collector of Tea Towels

Sue Couves
A Trip in 1977 : My Life So Far : No Looking Back : The Apple : The Beggar : The Tea Room at No. 84

Anthony Cowin
The Map
More about Anthony
Anthony Cowin is a writer and editor working within horror and sci-fi. He also writes reviews and articles for several genre magazines and websites.

Instagram and Twitter: @tonycowin

Jayne Curtis
Hearing Aide
More about Jayne
I live in Medway with the long suffering husband; it really is true that he talks to my handbag! I am currently editing my FBI thriller, which is growing into a series. Lots of ideas making my head hurt. The first title is 'Agent Allison - To Protect and Serve - Obsession'. Editing is quite hard, so it was some relief to have some fun in taking part in the 84 word challenge. I hope you enjoyed it. Right, back to the editing...

Em Dehaney
Liar Bird : Pecan Pie : Thunder
More about Em
Em Dehaney is a mother of two, a writer of fantasy and a drinker of tea. Born in Gravesend, her writing is inspired by the history of her home town. She is made of tea, cake, blood and magic. Her debut short story collection Food Of The Gods is available now on Amazon.

You can always find her at http://www.emdehaney.com/ or lurking about on Facebook posting pictures of witches https://www.facebook.com/emdehaney/

Debra Frayne
Wolf Moon

Jonathan Fryer
The Great Escape
More about Jonathan
I felt it important for people to appreciate that life begins before birth. These 84 words played with the idea that the unborn child might feel frustrated and could not wait to start afresh – something we all might feel, occasionally.

Email: fryerj@hotmail.co.uk

Ros Fryer
The Miracle

Peter Germany

Ghost : Immigrant : It Rained : Parrot : Priest : Support
: When I Grow Up
More about Peter
Peter Germany is a writer of Science Fiction and Horror
from Gravesend in Kent, England. He has had stories
published in the anthologies Sparks: An Electric
Anthology, 12 Days of Christmas 2017, and Under The
Weather.

Website: petergermany.com/

David John Griffin

Courage on an Anniversary : Elliot Delivers Groceries :
Extraordinary Event : Lashings of Custard : Last
Memories : Riot : Stranger on the Train : The Collector
: The Old Lady and Home Help
More about David
David John Griffin is a writer, graphic designer and app
designer. He lives in Gravesend, Kent with his wife
Susan, and two dogs called Bullseye and Jimbo. His first
three books were published by Urbane Publications: a
gothic novel called *The Unusual Possession of Alastair
Stubb*, a literary/psychological novel called *Infinite Rooms*,
and a magical realism/paranormal novella with short
stories called *Two Dogs At The One Dog Inn And Other
Stories*. He has stories published in three anthologies, one
of which was shortlisted for The HG Wells Short Story
competition 2012. He self-published a science fiction
adventure called *Abbie and the Portal* in 2018 and the
urban fantasy novel *Turquoise Traveller* in 2019.

Website: www.davidjohngriffin.com
Twitter: @MagicalRealized

Matt Hill

A Measure of Hate : Anti-social Behaviour : Gift Horse
: Jennifer : Parrot Strikes Back : Waiting in a Car
: Works Hard for the Money
More about Matt

Matt is a designer, a developer, and an infrequent writer.
He does some of these things for money, and some of
them for fun. One day he might get around to writing
that novel, but for now he's content to pen micro fictions:
short, sharp stories, often with a twist.

Find him on Twitter: @matthillco

Paul Hiscock

A Perfect Crime Scene
More about Paul

Paul is an author of crime, fantasy and science fiction
tales. His short stories have appeared in several
anthologies and include a seventeenth century
whodunnit, Sherlock Holmes stories and a science fiction
western. Paul lives with his family in Kent and spends his
days engaged in the far more challenging task of taking
care of his two children. He mainly does his writing in
coffee shops with members of the local NaNoWriMo
group or in the middle of the night when his family has
gone to sleep. Consequently, his stories tend to be fuelled
by large amounts of black coffee.

Website: www.detectivesanddragons.uk

Sam Jewiss
Football and Flowers
More about Sam
I am writer from Kent who loves writing YA. Especially urban fantasy and sci-fi YA.

Twitter and Instagram: @samjewiss

Lex H Jones
The Box
More about Lex
Lex H Jones is a British author, horror fan and rock music enthusiast who lives in North England.

Lex's noir crime novel "The Other Side of the Mirror" was published in 2019, with his first published novel "Nick and Abe" published in 2016. Lex also has a growing number of short horror stories published in themed anthologies.

He has written articles for premier horror websites the 'Gingernuts of Horror' and the 'Horrifically Horrifying Horror Blog' on various subjects covering books, films, videogames and music. When not working on his own writing Lex also contributes to the proofing and editing process for other authors.

Official Facebook page: www.facebook.com/LexHJones
Amazon author page:
https://www.amazon.co.uk/Lex-HJones/e/B008HSH9BA
Twitter: @LexHJones

Kayleigh Manley
Hello Beastie : Openings
More about Kayleigh

Even at a young age I wanted to create stories, but it's only been in the last 7 years or so that I've found the confidence to do so. Intrigued by the Paranormal, the Supernatural, and the psychology of human beings, I enjoy adding a touch of these elements into my writing.

I live on a narrowboat with my pet cat Poppy. My hobbies include buying new books and adding them to the ever-increasing pile of books I need to read, having an unhealthy obsession with Captain America and eating Chinese food.

Some of my favourite authors include Joe Hill, Patrick Ness, Lauren James and R. L Stine.

Instagram: @k.d.m_writtenwords
Twitter: @kayleighcakes1

Ben Morton
Farming philosophy : That Christmas feeling : Two Frogs – A Romance : Van Gogh
More about Ben
ALS IXH XAN

Email: bhmorton2@btinternet.com

Brenda Marlene Moss
Our Seasalter Holiday in Gran's Charabanc
More about Brenda
Married with two grown up daughters and three
grandchildren.

Born and lives in Gillingham.

Previously a voluntary Guide Leader for 20 years

Retired Community Co-ordinator (employed by a local
charity working with unemployed adults.)

Now enjoying family life, socialising, writing, painting
icons, and learning the banjo.

Is a member of Medway Mermaids and the Ramases
Society.

Email: brendamoss14@outlook.com.

Catriona Murfitt
She Left

Judith Northwood-Boorman
Happy Christmas Passengers
More about Judith
Judith always held a long standing ambition to teach
English and write a novel.

In 2003 she achieved her first ambition. She taught
"Communication Skills" to 16-17 year olds at West Kent
College for four months. But the temptation of knocking
a few heads together became just too great.

So after careers in management, primarily in business
travel and the dyslexia world, she took early retirement,
looking after in-laws with dementia.

Her two illustrated children's books raised over £12,000
for charity. Two poems have been published in separate
anthologies. She is a member of the women's writing
group, Medway Mermaids. Still working on the novel....

Website: https://joie-de-vivre-books.business.site/

Chrissie Pountain
The Park

Sally Skeptic
Number 84 : Regret : The Architect : The Lion

Dom Sullivan
People

Mike Swift

Courage : The Beginning

More about Mike

In the past, attended writing courses at Maidstone, Meopham and Sidcup. Several poems published in various anthologies and placed in writing competitions organised by the local library. Set up The Chapter & Verse Writing Group,which meets in Northfleet, in 1996.

Email: mikeswift@blueyonder.co.uk

Paolo Viscardi

Mummy Smell : Tea for Two? : Tea for Two? Reprise

More about Paolo

Paolo Viscardi is a natural history curator with a penchant for bones and science communication. He is more familiar with the smell of mummies than you might expect.

On Twitter as @PaoloViscardi

Richard Wall
Eighty-Four
More about Richard

Richard lives and writes in rural Worcestershire, but his stories reflect his life-long fascination with the dark underbelly of American culture; be it tales of the Wild West, the simmering menace of the Deep South, the poetry of Charles Bukowski, the writing of Langston Hughes or Andrew Vachss, or the music of Charley Patton, Son House, Johnny Cash, or Tom Waits.

A self-confessed Delta Blues music anorak, Richard embarked on a road trip from Memphis to New Orleans, where a bizarre encounter in Clarksdale, Mississippi inspired him to write his début novel, Fat Man Blues (https://richardwall.org/fat-man-blues/)

Richard's second novel, Last Rites at Sing Sing, is in the hands of his agent.

https://richardwall.org/ is where the magic happens.

Mark Whitehouse
Hospital Radio 1995
More about Mark

Graphic designer in love with irony, soulful mixtapes, Pilot fine liners, vermouth, Wes Anderson, Spanish cities, and all other graphic designer default settings.

Twitter: @so_mark

P Zakia
Aperture : Hot Chick : Ladysmith Black Mambazo :
Territorial : Wasteful Humans
More about P Zakia
P Zakia is an aspiring writer of science fiction, gothic
horror, fantasy, and occasionally cyber-fiction. She has
been known to dabble in short story writing. By day she
teaches English, where she works tirelessly to embed a
love of literature in her young charges. By night she
writes. Her dream is to be published and to give up her
day job. She lives in Kent and this will be her first work
in print.

Instagram: @pzakia_writes
Blog: www.mywordlyobsessions.wordpress.com
Writer's Blog:
www.notesaboutasmallisland.wordpress.com

THE ARTIST

Fitzy
Linea Portrait of No-One in 84 Individual Lines
More about Fitzy
My linea journey was broken 84 times by 84 visits to
number 84. Fragments of broken line began to form a
picture, 84 made it possible for me to break the line and
settle for a coffee whilst being creative.

Instagram: @Glennfitzy

44878701R00065

Printed in Poland
by Amazon Fulfillment
Poland Sp. z o.o., Wrocław